mary-kateandashley

TWO of a kind™

How to Flunk Your First Date

D1078473

Look for these

titles:

mary-kateandashley

How to Flunk Your First Date

adapted by Megan Stine

from the teleplay by Bob Keyes and Doug Keyes

from the series created by Robert Griffard
& Howard Adler

HarperCollins*Entertainment*

An Imprint of HarperCollins*Publishers*

A PARACHUTE PRESS BOOK

A PARACHUTE PRESS BOOK
Parachute Publishing, L.L.C.
156 Fifth Avenue
Suite 325
NEW YORK
NY 10010

First published in the USA by HarperEntertainment 1999
First published in Great Britain by Collins 2002
HarperCollins*Entertainment* is an imprint of HarperCollins*Publishers* Ltd,
77-85 Fulham Palace Road, Hammersmith, London W6 8JB

Cover photo by George Lange

The HarperCollins website address is
www.**fire**and**water**.com

7 9 8 6

ISBN 0 00 714479 2

Printed and bound in Great Britain by Clays Ltd, St Ives plc

CHAPTER ONE

"Whoa! Watch it!" Ashley Burke cried. She covered her blonde head with both arms to protect herself. Then she threw herself on the living-room couch. "You almost smacked me with the hockey puck!"

She aimed a pleading glance at her twin sister, Mary-Kate. "How did I ever let you talk me into this?" she wailed.

"Quit complaining. That puck couldn't have hurt you. It's just a balled-up sock!" Mary-Kate called. Ashley was such a wimp when it came to sports! "Come on! We're stomping them!"

Ashley and Mary-Kate were playing house hockey in the living room. It was three against three – girls against guys. Mary-Kate's team was fighting to the death against Max, Brian, and Brandon.

The boys were in the twins' seventh-grade class at school. Normally, any team with Ashley on it was doomed. She wasn't much of an athlete. Even super-athletic Mary-Kate couldn't make up for Ashley's butterfingers.

But the twins had a secret weapon – their babysitter, Carrie Moore.

Mary-Kate knew that she and Ashley were pretty old for a babysitter. After all, they were almost twelve! But the twins' mother died three years ago, and their father often had to teach late classes at the university where he was a professor. He wanted someone to be with the twins after school. That's where Carrie came in.

Carrie was the best babysitter the twins ever had. She was really easy to talk to. She knew how to shop till she dropped. She knew how to do cool stuff with her hair. And she knew how to handle boys.

She also happened to be a fabulous hockey player!

"Come on, Ashley!" Carrie called. "We're going to win this! Let's go!"

Ashley nervously glanced at Brandon, who had sent the 'puck' flying toward her head.

"Sorry about that," Brandon called sheepishly.

2

He waved his hockey stick in the air with a guilty grin. "I . . . uh . . . slipped."

"Come on, Ashley!" Mary-Kate yelled. "We're on a roll here. We've got to keep our rhythm going!"

"This is pitiful," Max moaned. "We're getting crushed by two girls and a babysitter!"

"Okay," Ashley agreed, hopping off the couch. "I'll get back in the game."

"All right!" Mary-Kate cheered. She tightened her grip on her hockey stick. Hockey wasn't normally her favourite sport – she was more of a basketball fan. But hockey was really fun to play indoors!
Carrie had pushed all the furniture to one end of the room. The goal was a big overstuffed armchair by the front door. Carrie had strapped two couch cushions to her legs, to use as shin guards.

"Okay," Carrie whispered as the three of them huddled at one end of the living room. "Here's the plan. Mary-Kate – you're going to be goalie now. And Ashley, you're going to score the next point. Throw a body check on Max, and I'll feed you the puck at centre ice. Got it?"

"A body check?" Ashley raised her eyebrows. "What's that, and how do I throw it?"

Mary-Kate held back an exasperated sigh. "Never mind. Just try to get open."

"Right," Ashley muttered half-heartedly.

Carrie flipped her bright red hair over her shoulders. She tugged on her grey sweatshirt. Then she crouched down in a face-off position with Max.

"Get ready, Max," she said, staring him right in the eyes. " 'Cause I'm going to roll right over you!"

Max gulped. Then Brian dropped the sock-puck on the floor.

BAM! Carrie's stick hit it first. She sent the puck flying towards Ashley, who was waiting in position to score.

"I've got it! I've got it!" Ashley cried excitedly.

No, she hasn't, Mary-Kate thought. She winced as she saw Max and Brian closing in on Ashley. Their hockey sticks jabbed in her direction.

"No, I haven't!" Ashley's voice sounded panicked. As fast as she could, she passed the puck to her super-sports-star sister.

"It's mine!" With one smooth move, Mary-Kate whacked the sock straight into the goal.

"Yeah!" Carrie cheered, shooting her fists into the air. "Great shot!"

All three girls started jumping up and down, yelling. Mary-Kate was cheering so hard, she didn't even notice when the front door swung open.

But then she spotted her father, Professor Kevin

Burke, standing in the doorway with his briefcase in his hand. She froze in the middle of a scream.

Uh-oh!

Dad wasn't supposed to be home for another half an hour!

Carrie had already stopped cheering. She put on a stern face.

"You kids have a lot of nerve, playing hockey in here!" she said. She waved a hand around the living room, which was a complete mess. "Honestly, you could break something!"

Carrie whirled – and pretended to spot Kevin for the first time.

"Oh, hi, Professor!" she said in a surprised voice.

Mary-Kate swallowed hard. She knew why Carrie wanted to stay on Kevin's good side. Not only did she work for him – she was also one of his students! Kevin taught her environmental studies class at the university.

"Hi, Carrie," Kevin said. A small smile crept across his lips. He stared at the couch cushions that were strapped to Carrie's legs. "Where did you get your hockey equipment? Sofas 'R' Us?"

Carrie's cheeks turned slightly red. She yanked off her shin guards.

"Uh, Max made me do it?" she said with a shrug.

"Me?" Max said. "Are you kidding?"

"Oh, don't act all innocent," Carrie scolded him. She turned back to Kevin. "Well, I suppose you want to give them a good talking to. I'll be in the kitchen."

With that, she hurried out of the room.

I hope Dad isn't mad, Mary-Kate thought, watching Carrie go. She knew that ever since Kevin had hired Carrie, he'd been wondering if she was the right person for the job. And it was true, sometimes Carrie acted more like a teenager than an adult. But that was part of what made her so great!

"Why are you home so early, Dad?" Ashley asked.

"Today was teacher conference day at your school. I had a conference with Miss Tandy," Kevin answered solemnly.

Mary-Kate's heart sank. "Uh-oh," she muttered. She had been worrying about this teacher conference for a week now. She knew she wasn't exactly the best student in the class. She didn't get all A's, the way Ashley did.

"This is going to get ugly," Brian announced, grabbing his hockey stick. "I'm out of here."

"Me too," Max said. "See you tomorrow, Ashley. See you in about a month, Mary-Kate!"

All three boys zoomed out the front door.

"Mary-Kate, remember that little talk we had

about maths?" Kevin began. He put his arm around his daughter and led her over to the couch. "Remember what I said?"

Mary-Kate gulped. "Uh, yeah, I remember," she replied. "You said, 'Don't worry – in real life you can always use a calculator.' Right, Dad?"

Ashley giggled. "Good one!"

Kevin smiled. "Nice try," he said. "But that's not what I said. I said that if you didn't improve, you'd be getting a tutor. Well, congratulations. Your tutor starts tomorrow after school."

"But Dad, I can't! I play basketball after school!" Mary-Kate protested. "And there's a big game coming up! If I don't show up at enough practices, I won't get to play. Coach Martin said anybody who misses five practices can't play in the game. He'll let Tanya Morris take my spot on the team!"

"Sorry, sweetheart, you've just been benched," Kevin replied. "At least until your grades improve. Now go on upstairs – and hit the books. Miss Tandy's giving you a make-up test on Friday."

Mary-Kate opened her mouth to argue some more. But her dad just shook his head.

Her shoulders slumped. She dragged herself off the couch and clomped up the stairs.

What a catastrophe!

Ashley followed her. "Cheer up," she whispered.

"How can I?" Mary-Kate answered. "I'm going to miss basketball every single day!"

"Only until your maths grades improve," Ashley argued.

"Oh, great! Only until I graduate, in that case!" Mary-Kate shot back. "You know what this means, Ashley? It means my life is over!"

CHAPTER TWO

"I wish we had time to talk more about oxygen and silicon," Kevin Burke said to his college class. He paced back and forth in front of the blackboard. "I'm sure you're all dying to know what mineral they form. But . . . "

He glanced at the clock in his classroom.

" . . . unfortunately, you'll have to live in suspense until next Thursday. Class is over. See you later."

Most of the students began shuffling their books and getting up to leave.

But Carrie Moore didn't budge. She was waiting for the room to clear out.

Professor Burke is really sort of good-looking, she thought. *And he's a nice guy – in his own way.*

I wonder why he never dates anyone?

Carrie stuffed her textbook into her leather backpack. Then she stood up and approached Kevin's desk.

He was straightening papers. He hardly noticed her.

"Professor?" Carrie began.

Kevin glanced up and smiled. "Okay, the answer is quartz," he said. "There. Now are you happy?"

Wow, Carrie thought. That was another thing about him. He was so brainy.

It was kind of cute, once you got used to it.

"No," she said with a laugh. "You wanted to see me – remember? You asked me to stay after class."

"Oh, right!" Kevin slapped his forehead. "I need to ask you a favour. Could you stay a little later with the girls tonight?"

"Sure." Carrie nodded. "Got a hot date?"

"No way! At least, I hope not!" Kevin laughed. "I'm just going out with my friend Eddie. I'll be home around eight."

"No problem," Carrie said.

Kevin started packing up his books. But Carrie just stood there, eyeing him up and down. Checking out his corduroy jeans. His brown hiking boots. His dimpled chin.

10

Not bad! she thought.

Finally he glanced up.

"Uh . . . did you want something?" he asked.

Carrie cleared her throat. "It's probably none of my business," she began. "But I've been working for you for a couple of weeks now and, well . . . do you ever date?"

"You're right. It's probably none of your business," Kevin said firmly. "See you tonight."

He walked towards the window ledge, where he'd left his clipboard.

He's trying to avoid the question, Carrie thought. *No way! I'm not letting him off the hook that easily!*

"I don't get it," she went on, following him and talking fast. "You're a good-looking guy with a decent job. You must get opportunities. Right?"

"Look, if you must know – and apparently you must," Kevin snapped, "I haven't had time to date. In the three years since my wife died, I've been too busy raising the girls."

"And you're doing a great job!" Carrie said quickly. "But now that I'm around, well, maybe it's time you got out."

Kevin turned away and hurried back to his desk. Carrie followed him.

"I know lots of women," she went on. "And I

love setting people up. What's your type? Brooding? Intellectual? Or do you just want someone who— "

Kevin held up his hand like a stop sign. "Look, when I meet someone I'm interested in, I'll ask her on a date myself."

"No, no, I really don't mind helping out!" Carrie insisted. "Glamorous? Earthy? Athletic?"

Kevin let out an exasperated sigh. "Would it help you if I wrote 'NO' on the board in capital letters?" he asked.

"All right, all right," Carrie said. Her shoulders slumped. "I'll butt out."

"Thank you," Kevin muttered, heading for the door.

"Although you'd love my friend Donna," she couldn't help adding. She followed him down the hall. "Five foot six, beautiful blue eyes . . . "

Ignoring her, Kevin strode quickly away, hurrying down the hall towards his office.

Finally Carrie quit trying to keep up with him. But she wasn't ready to drop the subject. Not yet.

"How do you feel about cats?" she called, her voice echoing in the hall. "Because I've got a friend with six Siamese kittens. Or are you a dog guy?"

No answer.

Oh, well, Carrie thought. *I'll give up – for now. But not forever!*

She gazed after Kevin as he disappeared into his office.

He's too much of a prize to stay single for long!

CHAPTER THREE

"Shh! He's coming!" Mary-Kate whispered to Ashley. "Don't say a thing!"

Mary-Kate was busy changing the hands on the mantel clock. She moved them forward twenty minutes. Then she dashed back to the dining table where all her school books were spread out.

Ashley shrugged. "I won't say a thing – because I won't be here," she declared. "I'm leaving. I'm not the one who needs a maths tutor."

"Well, if my plan works, I won't be here, either," Mary-Kate said, glancing again at the mantel clock. "I'll be at basketball practice – which started ten minutes ago."

A moment later Kevin strolled into the living

room with his oldest friend, Eddie Fairbanks. The two of them were followed by Carrie.

"Come on, Kevin," Eddie urged. He ran a hand impatiently through his short, dark hair. "Let's move it. I don't want to miss the monster truck demonstration."

"Let me get my coat," Kevin replied.

This is good, Mary-Kate thought. *Eddie wants to get out of here fast. And when he looks at the mantel clock, he'll be in even more of a hurry!*

"So – where are you two going?" Carrie asked, her hands on her hips.

Don't slow them down! Mary-Kate pleaded silently. *Or my plan will never work!*

"We're doing a little male bonding," Eddie answered. "We're going to the auto show." He glanced at the clock. "Oh, man, we're late already!"

Yes! Mary-Kate wanted to cheer. So far, so good.

"Oh! So is one of you buying a car?" Carrie's face lit up.

"You don't buy a car at the auto show," Eddie informed her.

"So what do you do? Test drive some of the new models?" Carrie asked.

Eddie made a face. "No. They don't let you do that."

Carrie threw up her hands. Her blue nail polish sparkled.

"Okay, I don't get it," she declared. "What's with guys and the auto show, anyway?"

"Are you kidding? It's a blast! You buy a hot dog, you walk around . . . " Eddie explained.

"And you look at all the cars you can't afford, with all the other guys who can't afford them!" Kevin chimed in.

"Can't you do the same thing in a parking lot and save fifteen bucks?" Carrie challenged them.

Kevin shook his head. "It wouldn't be the same," he announced. Then he glanced at Eddie to check. "Would it?"

"No way," Eddie declared. "Look, it's just something we do, okay? Like the way you women get all excited about Tupperware."

Uh-oh! Mary-Kate didn't like the way Carrie's eyes were starting to flash. She might keep them here, arguing, forever!

Then Eddie turned to Kevin. "Can we go before she sucks all the fun out of it?"

Carrie rolled her eyes. "Don't let me hold you up," she said, and went back into the kitchen.

Kevin slipped on his coat.

Now's my chance, Mary-Kate thought. She

16

glanced at the clock one more time.

"Dad, I don't know about this tutor guy," she began. "It's his first day, and he's ten minutes late already!" She pointed at the mantel. "I say we dump him."

Her dad didn't even blink. He just calmly checked his watch. Then he turned the hands on the mantel clock back twenty minutes.

"Nice try," he told her. "I'll let you reset the clock in the kitchen."

Oh, man! Mary-Kate thought. *Don't I get any breaks? It looks like I'm going to be stuck here all afternoon. Doing maths!*

"It was worth a shot," Ashley whispered to her sister. "Well, I'm going over to Jessica's," she announced. "We're going to watch her mom wax her eyebrows."

"Even that sounds good!" Mary-Kate moaned.

"Wow. You must be desperate!" Ashley replied. "You hate all that make-up stuff!"

Kevin folded his arms. "The only make-up you should be worrying about, Mary-Kate, is the make-up test on Friday," he said in a firm voice.

Mary-Kate rolled her eyes.

"Well, I'm gone," Ashley said. She headed for the front door. Just as she reached for the doorknob, there was a knock. She flung the front door open.

A boy in a white T-shirt, jeans, and sunglasses stood on the stoop. His brown hair was streaked with gold. He reached up casually and pulled off his sunglasses, revealing sky-blue eyes.

Even Mary-Kate could see that he was a serious hunk. Fabulous-looking. Although, as far as she was concerned, boys were only good for playing hockey and shooting hoops with.

"Hey, I'm Taylor, the maths guy," he announced to Ashley. "Are you Mary-Kate?"

Ashley just stood there for a second, staring at him.

"Uh . . . let me think . . . " she said in a dreamy voice. Mary-Kate took one glance at the goofy expression on Ashley's face, and she knew the truth.

Ashley had a crush on Taylor. Big time.

Oh, brother! Mary-Kate thought. *This could be a big mess!*

All Mary-Kate wanted was to get rid of this maths tutor. Then she could practise basketball every day. She could keep her slot on the team – and make sure she got to play in the big game.

But from the look on her sister's face, she could tell: Ashley would do anything to spend time with Taylor!

And that meant that if Mary-Kate was going to get rid of Taylor, she'd have to do it alone!

CHAPTER FOUR

Kevin stepped forward. "Hi, Taylor," he said pleasantly. "I'm Kevin Burke. This is my daughter Ashley. And that's Mary-Kate." He pointed towards Mary-Kate.

Rats! Mary-Kate thought.

Taylor glanced back and forth from Mary-Kate to Ashley, looking slightly confused.

"Whoa," he said. "I hope you don't think you're getting a two-for-one deal here."

Kevin laughed. "No, you'll only be tutoring Mary-Kate."

"Okay, fine," Taylor said. "I get ten bucks an hour, a ten-minute break every session, and I don't do logarithms."

Kevin nodded. "Seems fair."

"Very fair," Ashley gushed.

"Can we go now?" Eddie asked impatiently.

"Have a good session," Kevin called to Mary-Kate as Eddie pushed him out the door.

Mary-Kate gulped. Okay. This was it. Face-to-face with the enemy.

"So," Taylor said, grinning at her. "I hear you're having trouble with fractions."

Mary-Kate opened her mouth to reply. But Ashley was already speaking.

"I personally love fractions," her sister blurted. "They're so useful. For example, I'm twelve and a quarter."

Mary-Kate stared at Ashley. She couldn't believe it. Her sister was lying about her age!

"And I'm guessing you are . . . fourteen and seven-eighths?" Ashley went on with a little giggle.

Excuse me while I gag, Mary-Kate thought. This was too much. Now Ashley was actually batting her eyelashes at Taylor!

Taylor screwed up his face.

"She's not going to be hanging around, is she?" he asked Mary-Kate.

"No way. I thought you were going to Jessica's," Mary-Kate said to her sister.

Ashley flipped her blonde hair off her neck. "I changed my mind," she announced. Then, looking only at Taylor, she said, "I'll be upstairs... if anybody needs me."

Then go! Mary-Kate thought. *The longer you hang around here, the longer this will take!*

Ashley started up the stairs backwards – so she could still stare and smile at Taylor as she went up.

"It was a pleasure meeting you, Taylor," she began. "I hope I— aaahh!"

Ashley missed her footing – and sat down hard on the steps. Mary-Kate clapped a hand to her mouth, trying not to laugh. She didn't want to embarrass Ashley or anything – but her sister looked so ridiculous!

"I'm okay!" Ashley said quickly. Her cheeks turned pink. "Don't get up! Happy tutoring."

She hurried up the rest of the steps – forward. The normal way.

"What's her story?" Taylor asked when Ashley was gone.

"You haven't got the time," Mary-Kate said with a sigh. "Take my word for it!"

Taylor laughed. Picking up Mary-Kate's maths book, he opened it and began to leaf through it.

"Oh, wow," he said, turning the pages slowly.

"I remember this book. We had it in Miss Tandy's class."

"Miss Tandy?" Mary-Kate's eyes popped open. "You had her, too? I'm in her class this year."

"Yeah." Taylor nodded. "We had a blast in there. She's a fun teacher."

"Fun? Are you kidding?" Mary-Kate cried. "She's a slave driver! She piles on the homework every night – even on Fridays!"

"Yeah, I know," Taylor agreed. "But you've got to remember. She's a Tootsie Pop."

"A Tootsie Pop?" Mary-Kate frowned. "I don't get it."

"Hard on the outside," Taylor explained, "but soft and sweet in the middle. We used to call her 'Tootsie' behind her back. Hey – does she still have that basketball hoop hanging up over the chalkboard?"

"Yes," Mary-Kate said. "But she goes ballistic if anyone tries to shoot baskets – even with balled-up wads of paper! No one can figure out what she has it for, anyway."

"Just wait until the end of the year," Taylor said with a twinkle in his eye.

"Why? What happens then?"

"Promise you won't tell anyone else?"

"Sure." Mary-Kate nodded. "Promise."

"At the end of the year, she lets you tear all the pages out of your maths and science workbooks," Taylor said. "Then you get to wad them up – and shoot baskets all day!"

"Cool!" Mary-Kate said. She reached up and slapped Taylor a high five.

"Yeah, it's cool," he agreed, giving her a smile. "Hang in there. Miss Tandy isn't so bad."

Taylor picked up a pencil. "Well, then," he said, "if you're going to shoot a lot of end-of-the-year baskets, you want to rack up as many pages of maths homework as you can."

Mary-Kate nodded glumly. "I guess so." Then she turned to her maths book with a sigh.

Taylor was nice. For a tutor.

But shooting end-of-the-year baskets was not on the top of her list. Neither was sitting around talking about fractions. What she really wanted, more than anything, was to be working on her jump shot right now. So that Coach Martin wouldn't give her spot on the team to Tanya Morris!

I hate this, Mary-Kate thought. *By the time I get my maths grades up, I'll be shooting free throws worse than Shaq!*

I've got to think of a way to get out of this tutoring thing – and fast!

CHAPTER FIVE

Mary-Kate trudged up the stairs to her room. Her head was spinning with numbers. Fractions. Decimals. Percents.

How come Ashley got all the brains in the maths department? she wondered. It didn't seem fair, considering they were twins.

Although they weren't identical twins. That much was obvious. All you had to do was glance at Ashley's side of the room, with its white four-poster bed neatly covered by a pink flowered quilt, to see how different the twins were. Mary-Kate's side was decorated with sports posters and trophies. The oversize Chicago Cubs T-shirt that she slept in was tossed carelessly over the footboard of her bed.

Ashley was lying on her bed, flipping through a magazine. She leaped up when Mary-Kate walked in.

"Did Taylor leave already?" she demanded. "I wanted to say goodbye."

"He's gone. But he'll be back tomorrow," Mary-Kate said glumly.

"Did he say anything about me?" Ashley asked eagerly.

"Yeah. He said with all the sodas you came down to get, you must have a bladder the size of Lake Michigan!" Mary-Kate answered.

Ashley beamed. "So he did notice me," she cooed.

Mary-Kate rolled her eyes and flopped down on her own bed. She wasn't in the mood to talk about boys right now.

Ashley hurried over and sat down beside her.

"Listen," she said in an excited voice, "what if I told you I might have a way to get you back on the basketball court every day after school?"

Mary-Kate sat up fast.

"Are you kidding? I'd be willing to call you Your Royal Highness – for a week!" she said. "How?"

Ashley lowered her voice. "We could switch places – and I could go to your tutoring sessions," she suggested.

Mary-Kate stared at Ashley. "You mean you'd

really do that?" she asked, amazed.

"Of course. You're my twin sister," Ashley said. "When you suffer, I suffer. I couldn't stand for you to get kicked off the basketball team – right before the big game!"

"Yeah, right," Mary-Kate cracked. "Don't lie – you've got a thing for Taylor, haven't you?"

"He is so gorgeous!" Ashley burst out. "Didn't you notice?"

"I noticed," Mary-Kate admitted.

Ashley nudged Mary-Kate with her shoulder. "So . . . what do you say?"

What do I say? Mary-Kate thought. It took her about half a second to make up her mind.

"Gee, let's see. You have to study maths, while I get to play basketball?" Mary-Kate pretended to weigh the choices. "I say . . . it works for me!"

"Great!" Ashley cried. She twirled joyfully around the room. Then she flopped down on her bed. She stared up at the ceiling with a happy smile on her face.

"And she's supposed to be the smart one," Mary-Kate muttered, shaking her head.

"I heard that," Ashley said. She sat up again. "I am the smart one. And that's why I think we'd better plan this out."

"Plan it? What's to plan?" Mary-Kate asked.

"What we're going to wear. What we'll say. How to act," Ashley explained. "We've got to practise. Because we're going to have to fool everyone."

Mary-Kate nodded. "True." She bit her lip. "You know, Dad will never fall for it. He can always tell us apart. Remember when we switched name tags for the baseball game? He wasn't fooled for a second. And if he finds out about this, he'll ground us for life. Or more!"

"Right," Ashley agreed. "That's why we have to make sure Dad never sees us. Ever. And we're going to have to be very careful around Carrie, too."

Mary-Kate paced around the room. They'd be in so much trouble if they got caught! Was it really worth the risk?

Yes! she decided at last. *I'll do anything to play in the big game!*

She took a deep breath. "Okay – I'm up for it."

Then she thought of something else. She glanced nervously at Ashley's closet. "Wait a second. What do I have to wear?" she asked with a gulp.

"Hmmm . . . " Ashley stared into her own closet.

Mary-Kate saw the sneaky twinkle in her sister's eyes.

"No. No way. Not the D word!" Mary-Kate said.

"You said it, I didn't," Ashley declared. "Yes. You have to wear – a dress!"

Mary-Kate flinched. How was she supposed to play basketball in a dress? She couldn't. It was impossible.

But she knew Ashley was right. To fool Carrie into thinking she was Ashley, she'd have to dress like Ashley.

"I'll wear this to school tomorrow," Ashley said. She pulled an extra-feminine flowered dress out of her closet. "My favourite dress, with tights to match and a bow in my hair. You'll wear – whatever it is you wear."

"The usual," Mary-Kate chimed in. "Blue jeans, a T-shirt, my baseball cap."

"Ugh," Ashley said, making a face. "See what I'm willing to go through for you?"

"For Taylor – not for me!" Mary-Kate corrected her.

Ashley shrugged. "Anyway, we can trade outfits in school," she said. "So when we come home, we'll be wearing each other's clothes. Carrie will think you're me, and she'll let you leave. You can beat it out of here to your basketball practice. No one will even blink!"

"I'll have to take some sweats with me to the practice," Mary-Kate muttered. "I mean, you don't expect me to shoot free throws in that thing! Do you?"

She wrinkled her nose at the flowered dress.

"No way!" Ashley agreed. "That's one of my hottest outfits. Don't you dare play basketball with it on! I just wish Taylor could see me in it."

"Well, look at it this way," Mary-Kate said. "He'll see me in it – but he'll think it's you. Right?"

Ashley thought about it for a moment. "I guess. Somehow it doesn't seem the same, though," she added with a frown.

Mary-Kate picked up her maths book and handed it to Ashley. "Here – we'd better trade books, too. Otherwise he might notice that the wrong name is in the front."

"Whatever," Ashley said, gazing off into the distance with a dreamy look. "I just can't wait for tomorrow."

Me either, Mary-Kate thought. *Tomorrow after school, I'll get back on the basketball court. I can finally start to live again!*

If we can pull this switch off!

CHAPTER SIX

Kevin stepped into his favourite coffee bar the next morning. He breathed in deeply. He loved the smell of coffee.

"Morning, Kevin," the pretty young woman behind the counter said. "The usual – a blueberry muffin and a large house blend? Coming up!"

"Thanks, Stephanie," Kevin said, flashing her a smile.

This is nice, he thought. Coming in here every morning before class. Sipping coffee. Getting ready to start the day. He liked his routine.

"Good morning, Professor," a voice behind him chirped.

Kevin froze. He knew that voice. And it was not

a voice he wanted to hear with his morning coffee!

"Carrie," he groaned, turning around.

It wasn't that he disliked Carrie. Not at all. She was a decent student, and she was turning out to be a pretty good babysitter, too. And, he had to admit to himself, he actually found her funny.

But did she have to show up everywhere he went?

"Can I get that to go?" he called to Stephanie, who was pouring his coffee.

"No problem," Stephanie called back.

Carrie frowned just a little when she heard the words "to go".

She looks as if she knows I'm trying to get away from her, Kevin thought. That made him feel guilty. He didn't want to hurt her feelings.

It was just that Carrie was so . . . out there. Always saying exactly what she thought. Blunt and to the point.

The annoying thing was, half the time, she was right!

He watched Carrie step up to the counter and stare into the pastry case.

"Uh, what's that big sticky-looking thing?" Carrie asked Stephanie.

"That would be our sticky bun," Stephanie

answered. She and Kevin shared an amused glance as she wrapped up his muffin.

"I don't suppose it's low-fat?" Carrie asked.

"Sure it is – compared to a slab of ribs," Stephanie joked.

Carrie grinned. "Well, then, what are you waiting for? Warm it up!"

Kevin laughed out loud. Okay – he had to admit it. He sort of liked how free Carrie was. How she took chances and just did things. It wasn't his style at all – but he had to admire it.

Stephanie put the pastry in the microwave. Then she handed Kevin his coffee and muffin to go.

"Hey – is that a new jacket?" Stephanie asked him. She reached over the counter and touched the sleeve of his tweed blazer.

"I must be drinking too much coffee if you're noticing new pieces in my wardrobe," Kevin joked.

"It's a good colour on you," Stephanie told him.

"Really? You like it?" Kevin felt his cheeks getting warm. "Uh . . . thanks. See you later."

He picked up his coffee and carried it over to the cream-and-sugar bar. Carrie followed him.

"She's cute," Carrie said softly. She gestured in Stephanie's direction with her head.

"Stephanie?" Kevin glanced back at her. Her

long, silky brown hair hung over her shoulders. She had large, green eyes and a slim figure. "Yeah, I guess she is."

"So what are you going to do about it?" Carrie asked.

"What do you mean?" Kevin asked warily. In fact, he had a feeling he knew exactly what Carrie meant – but he hoped he was wrong.

"You said when you found someone you were attracted to, you'd ask her out," Carrie reminded him.

When did I say that? Kevin wondered.

Then he remembered. The other day after class.

When Carrie was hounding him about dating someone.

I should have known that would come back to haunt me! he thought.

"Carrie, I appreciate your interest," Kevin began, trying to be nice. Then he changed his mind. Maybe honesty would work better. "Actually, come to think of it, I don't."

"She obviously likes you," Carrie whispered, ignoring the hint.

"Look, I don't—" Kevin began. Then he stopped. Did he hear Carrie right?

"She likes me?" He kept his voice low, too.

Carrie nodded and motioned for him to follow her. She led him to a seat at a table by the wall. She chose one that was far away from the counter, so they could talk without Stephanie overhearing.

Carrie leaned over the table towards Kevin. "Of course she likes you!" she declared. "Are you kidding? The way she knew your coffee order? The way she complimented you on your clothes?"

"She was just making conversation," Kevin argued. He took a sip of his coffee.

Carrie stared at him as if he were an alien.

"Right," she said. "She was making conversation. And the conversation was: 'Hel-lo. I like you.' Didn't you get that?"

Kevin shook his head. He wasn't buying it.

"Professor, it's not what a person says, but how they say it," Carrie went on. "Most communication is nonverbal."

"Except, of course, in your case," Kevin chimed in.

Carrie ignored the dig. "I'm telling you, she's sending you major signals," she insisted.

Kevin stared at her. Could it be? Could Carrie be right about this?

Maybe she is, he thought. *Eddie always says women know about these things.*

"Tell you what," Carrie said. She picked up an empty paper coffee cup. "If I sink this in that trash can over there, you ask her out."

Kevin eyed the trash can. It was about twenty feet away. Could she make it? It was a long shot—

Wait a second! What was he thinking?

"Why would I go along with that?" he asked.

"Because it's an impossible shot," Carrie replied. She opened her eyes wide at him. "There's no way I can make it."

Kevin sighed. What was it about Carrie that made him get involved in stuff like this? She made him act like a kid again – and he just couldn't seem to say no to her.

"Okay," he agreed, giving in. "But if I take this bet, then will you let me leave?"

"Absolutely!" Carrie promised.

Kevin scooted back his chair to move out of Carrie's way.

"Go for it," he said, nodding towards the trash can.

With her arm raised, Carrie easily tossed the cup the length of the coffee bar. It fell straight into the trash without even touching the sides. A perfect shot.

Kevin shook his head. "Okay, let's hear it. How on earth did you manage that?" he asked. "I thought you said it was an impossible shot."

"I sit here every day," Carrie confessed with a shrug. "I haven't missed that shot in two weeks."

Kevin nodded. "It figures," he murmured.

"Well, it's your move, Professor," Carrie said. "Go on – ask her out."

Kevin glanced over at Stephanie again. He felt his palms start to sweat. Ask her out? Now?

Come on! It's not that big a deal, he told himself. "Okay. If it means that much to you, I'll ask her out," he said to Carrie.

He swallowed hard and stood up.

Here I go, he thought.

But he couldn't do it. He couldn't make his legs walk over to the counter. He felt like a teenager all over again.

Only, when he was a teenager, it wasn't this hard!

"I'll ask her out – the very next time I come in here!" he added.

Then he grabbed his coffee and muffin and raced quickly for the door.

"Chicken!" Carrie called after him.

As he hurried by the counter, Kevin saw Stephanie staring at Carrie with a confused expression.

"Crossword puzzle," Carrie explained. "He needed a seven-letter word for poultry."

Kevin couldn't help grinning at Carrie's fast cover-up as he slipped out the door. *She's really very funny*, he thought.

And maybe she's right, too.

Maybe Stephanie does like me.

Anyway, it wouldn't hurt to give it a try and ask her out.

Would it?

CHAPTER SEVEN

"Hold still, Mary-Kate," Ashley said. She brushed Mary-Kate's hair, pulling it away from her face. "Carrie has to believe that you're me. So I have to make you look extra pretty!"

She stepped back to study her work. Hmmm, not quite right. Reaching up, she fluffed Mary-Kate's fringe with her fingers. Then she leaned over Mary-Kate's shoulder and gazed at their reflections in the mirror of the girls' bathroom.

Mary-Kate rolled her eyes. She squirmed in the flowered dress.

The two girls had just changed clothes. They switched outfits in the school bathroom right after their last class.

"Ashley, how can you wear this thing?" Mary-Kate complained. "I feel like I'm late for a tea party at Barbie's Dreamhouse."

"Tough luck," Ashley retorted. "Look what your stupid baseball hat is doing to my hair. I'm losing all my bounce!"

"Hey, you're the one who wanted to switch places," Mary-Kate said.

"You wanted it, too!" Ashley shot back. "I'm saving your skin. Otherwise, you're off the basketball team for the big game – remember?"

"Yeah, but it was your idea," Mary-Kate said. "And you'd better hope this works, or you're going to be in big trouble."

Ashley stopped brushing her sister's hair. "Me? I thought we were in this together!"

"Oh, we are," Mary-Kate said. "Unless we get caught. Then you're on your own!"

Ashley yanked the brush through Mary-Kate's hair one more time. Hard.

"Ow!" Mary-Kate protested.

"See how we suffer for beauty?" Ashley laughed. "Those of us who even bother to try, that is."

"Watch it, Ashley," Mary-Kate threatened. "Or I'll go to the tutoring session myself – and you won't get to spend a single second with Taylor!"

"Okay, okay," Ashley agreed quickly. She put the finishing touches on Mary-Kate's hair. "Now let's go home and see if this works. If we can fool Carrie, we can sure fool Taylor."

The two girls hurried home. Carrie was sitting on the living-room couch with her feet up, drinking tea.

"Oh, that's a pretty dress, Ashley!" Carrie said when the two girls walked in.

"Thanks," Ashley answered automatically.

Mary-Kate nudged Ashley in the ribs.

"Uh, I mean, isn't it a nice dress?" Ashley fumbled. "Of course it's not something that I, Mary-Kate, would wear. But then, I don't have Ashley's incredible fashion sense."

Is she buying it? Or did I just blow it big time? Ashley wondered. She studied Carrie's face.

Carrie looked confused. But not suspicious.

Phew! That was a close one, Ashley thought.

"Well, what are you up to this afternoon, Ashley?" Carrie asked, raising her eyebrows at Mary-Kate.

Mary-Kate didn't reply. She was fiddling with the collar of her dress. "This thing is choking me," she grumbled.

"Ashley?" Carrie said again.

40

No answer. Ashley wanted to kick Mary-Kate – but she couldn't. Not with Carrie watching!

"Earth to Ashley," Carrie called. She waved her hand in front of Mary-Kate's face.

Mary-Kate jumped. "Oh! Uh . . . right!" she said, snapping out of it. "Well, uh, you know me. I thought I'd go over to Jessica's. She wants to, uh, do her hair like one of the Spice Girls."

Good answer! Ashley thought. *Finally!*

"Which one?" Carrie asked, sounding interested.

"Uh . . . Shorty?" Mary-Kate guessed.

Ashley winced. Her sister didn't know the Spice Girls from a cinnamon bun!

"You mean Sporty?" Carrie asked.

"Right, Sporty," Mary-Kate agreed quickly. "Not Shorty." She shook her head. "I always get those two mixed up."

Ashley felt like burying her head in her hands.

Carrie looked very puzzled. But before she could say anything else, the doorbell rang.

"That must be Taylor!" Ashley blurted out. "I'll get it!"

She flew to the front door and opened it.

"Hi," she breathed, gazing into Taylor's blue eyes. Oh, he was so cute! She could barely stand it!

"Uh, hi," Taylor said. He tossed a wadded-up

41

piece of paper at Ashley. It hit her lightly on the forehead. "Here – I saved this for you," he told her. "To add to your collection for the end of the year."

"Huh?" Ashley stared at him, confused. Mary-Kate was collecting crumpled-up pieces of paper? How weird!

Mary-Kate hurried over to the door. "Uh, that's so nice of you, Taylor!" she said quickly. "So when Miss Tandy lets us shoot baskets with our maths homework at the end of the year, you, Mary-Kate, will get some extra shots!" She dug her elbow into Ashley's ribs. "Remember?"

Ow! Ashley tried not to wince. *Shoot baskets? With our maths homework? What are they talking about?* she wondered.

But she nodded, pretending to understand. Whatever. Mary-Kate could explain it all later.

Right now, Ashley just wished that Mary-Kate would hurry up and leave. So she could be alone with Taylor.

And then, if she could get up the nerve, she was going to do something really daring. She'd been planning it all day.

She was going to ask Taylor to go out with her – on a date!

"So, well, goodbye, Ashley," Ashley said, trying

to hurry her sister.

"Uh, yeah. I'm off to Jessica's," Mary-Kate said.

She started to reach for the door. But then she stopped, snapping her fingers.

"Whoops! My, uh, bag of make-up," Mary-Kate said. "Jessica and I are going to do our eyes like the Spice Girls, too."

Make-up bag? No way, Ashley thought. *She's getting her sweats. For basketball.*

Mary-Kate ran upstairs. A second later, she came back down with a large plastic bag stuffed with something bulky.

"Wow!" Carrie exclaimed. "That's all make-up?"

"Uh, Jessica has really big eyes," Mary-Kate blurted out.

Then she hurried out the door.

Whew! Ashley thought. *That was close!*

Ashley led Taylor into the kitchen. They spread out her maths homework on the table. Taylor started going over it.

He is so cute! Ashley thought, staring at his profile as he studied her workbook. *And he's barely even three years older than I am. That's nothing!*

"Wow," Taylor said, glancing up at her. "I don't get it, Mary-Kate. Yesterday it was like you weren't even listening. But somehow you got every one of

43

these problems right!"

Ashley smiled dreamily at him.

"I think you underestimate what a good teacher you are," she said.

Taylor looked thoughtful. "Maybe so," he agreed. "Hey – maybe I'm not charging your father enough! I mean, even your handwriting has improved – right down to these little hearts you used for decimal points!"

"I was hoping you'd notice them," Ashley gushed. Taylor stared at her workbook again. "I'm impressed, Mary-Kate. I really am." He gave her a warm smile.

Yes! Ashley felt her heart beat faster. *I think he likes me!*

Taylor glanced at the kitchen clock. "Well, I guess we can move on to the next chapter," he suggested.

"Let me just scoot my chair a little closer to you," Ashley said.

Taylor gave her a funny look.

"So I can read over your shoulder," she added quickly.

She moved her chair so close, she could practically read the laundry instructions on the inside label of his T-shirt!

"Uh, okay – chapter four?" Taylor asked.

"Whatever you think," Ashley said adoringly.

"I'm yours for the next two hours."

"Yeah, great," Taylor said, leaning away. "But do you mind backing off a little?"

He's shy! That's so cute! Ashley thought. She moved her chair back. But just an inch or two. How could she stand to be more than a few feet away from him?

He was the perfect guy. Cute. Smart. Nice.

And between 3:30 and 5:30 every afternoon – he was hers!

Now all she had to do was get up the nerve to ask him for a real date!

CHAPTER EIGHT

"What time is Dad coming home?" Mary-Kate asked.

It was late that afternoon. She and Carrie were sitting in the kitchen, playing cards. It was a gambling game called '21'. They were using pennies from Carrie's purse to make bets.

Carrie knew all kinds of games like that. Before she moved to Chicago, she spent some time as a card dealer in Las Vegas. Just another of the many things that made her such a cool babysitter!

Ashley stood at the sink, back in her regular clothes. She was supposed to be drying the dishes – but every time she thought of the way Taylor smiled at her during their maths session, her dish towel would stop moving.

I think he really likes me! she thought. *I didn't have the nerve to ask him out today – but I'm definitely going to do it tomorrow!*

"Your dad should be here soon," Carrie answered Mary-Kate. "Why do you want to know?"

"Because I'm betting he won't like the fact that you're teaching us how to gamble," Mary-Kate commented.

"It's a form of maths," Carrie argued. "Besides, you're supposed to be betting on the cards – not on your dad. Now pay attention. I dealt. What do you want to do?"

"Hit me," Mary-Kate decided.

"Okay," Carrie said, dealing her a new card. "A nine. But see, if you'd doubled down, you would have made twice the money."

"Doubled down? What's that?" Mary-Kate asked.

Who cares? Ashley thought. She gave a happy sigh. *Who cares about anything but love?*

"It's when your first two cards total nine," Carrie began, "and then— "

She broke off as Kevin and Eddie walked into the kitchen.

"Whoops!" Mary-Kate muttered. "Busted!"

"Well, I'm pretty much go-fished out for the day!" Carrie said, quickly putting down the deck of cards.

Kevin leaned over the table and studied the cards.

"I hope you doubled down on that one, Mary-Kate," he said with a straight face.

Ashley grinned. *Dad may seem out of it sometimes – but he really doesn't miss much,* she thought.

"I was just helping her with her maths skills," Carrie explained.

"Makes sense to me," Eddie volunteered.

"Speaking of maths, how did the tutoring go today?" Kevin asked.

"Fabulous!" Ashley accidentally blurted out.

Kevin's head snapped in her direction. "How would you know?" he asked.

Whoops! "Uh, M-Mary-Kate told me," Ashley stammered. "I take an interest in her schoolwork, you know."

"That's right," Mary-Kate chimed in. "We're twins, Dad. We share everything. And that's why I'm going to show Ashley some of the really fascinating things I learned about decimals – right now! Aren't I, Ashley?"

Ashley nodded and put down her dish towel. The two of them left the kitchen in a rush.

Kevin stared after his daughters. *What was that all about?* he wondered. *They're acting as if they're up to something.*

He shrugged. Whatever it was, he was sure he'd find out about it sooner or later.

"Well, looks like Taylor's earning his money," he commented to Carrie.

"Mmm-hmmm," Carrie agreed. She began to gather the cards up from the table. Kevin watched her stuff them back in their pack. Her hands worked quickly and skilfully.

When the cards were put away, Carrie narrowed her eyes at Kevin.

"So? Did you ask her out?" she demanded.

"Ask who out?" Eddie quizzed. He raised his eyebrows.

"This woman he has a thing for," Carrie answered.

Kevin flinched. "A 'thing'? I hardly know her!" he protested.

"You have a 'thing' and I don't know about it?" Eddie looked hurt. "I'm supposed to be your best friend!"

"Carrie's talking about a girl who works at our coffee place. That's all," Kevin explained.

"You two have a coffee place?" Eddie cried. "We go back twenty years, you and I. And we don't have a coffee place!" He folded his arms. "Maybe next year you'd like to take Carrie to the auto show!"

Kevin threw up his hands. "Will you listen to

yourself? You sound like a kid!" he scolded.

"Excuse me," Carrie called. She rapped on the table with the deck of cards. "Can we get back on track here?" She turned to Kevin. "Look, did you ask Stephanie out – or not?"

"I was about to," Kevin admitted. "But then I felt stupid. I mean, asking a woman who works at a coffee bar to go out for coffee."

Carrie slapped her forehead. "Then take her clog dancing! Who cares? Just do something. This woman is sending you signals like crazy!"

Eddie's eyes lit up. "She's sending him signals?"

Carrie nodded. "Like you wouldn't believe."

"What's the matter with you?" Eddie said, swatting Kevin with the back of his hand. "Ask her out!"

Kevin snorted. He couldn't believe he was actually having this conversation!

"I'm a little nervous, okay?" he said. He paced back and forth. "I haven't asked a woman out since before Jan and I got married."

Carrie shrugged. "So you're a little rusty," she said. "So what? Just ask her to dinner."

Dinner? Kevin thought. *Yeah. Maybe . . .*

"No, no, no," Eddie jumped in. "Your instincts were right with the coffee date. I mean, what if she's really crazy?"

"She's not crazy," Kevin argued.

"But if she is – or maybe she's boring – you're going to want to make a quick exit," Eddie said. "That's why you need this."

He took a small black device out of his pocket and handed it to Kevin.

"What is it?" Kevin asked.

"A self-paging beeper," Eddie explained. "Let's say you're out with her. It starts to feel like the night's never going to end. So what do you do? Just hit this button and the beeper goes off."

"Really?" Kevin asked. He fiddled with the beeper buttons. "Then what?"

"Then you claim it's an emergency and – bingo! You're home watching TV in no time!" Eddie grinned.

Carrie jumped up and gave them both a dirty look.

"This is ridiculous!" she cried. "You haven't even asked her out yet – and you're already trying to find a way to dump her!"

"That's what guys do," Eddie agreed with a shrug.

Kevin felt himself blush.

"No, we don't," he protested. "We don't just dump women. Not all of us, anyway."

"Eddie," Carrie said in her nastiest voice, "it's

hard to believe that you need a beeper to get rid of women!"

Eddie glared at Kevin. "Are you going to let her talk to me like that?" he demanded.

"She's absolutely right," Kevin said firmly. "The first step is to ask Stephanie out. After that, I'll just play it by ear."

"Good," Carrie said, nodding triumphantly. She picked up her bag and marched towards the front door. "You won't be sorry, Professor. I'm sure of it. Just wait and see."

She walked out and pulled the door shut behind her.

Yes, Kevin thought. He could probably work up the guts to ask Stephanie out. It might even be fun. To start dating again.

But what if he didn't like her?

Or worse yet – what if she didn't like him?

He picked up the beeper again and turned to Eddie.

"So how did you say this thing worked?" he asked.

CHAPTER NINE

"Mary-Kate, please," Ashley begged her sister as they were getting dressed the next morning. "Please don't wear that ratty old jersey with the holes in it. I want to look especially nice when Taylor comes over after school today."

"Why?" Mary-Kate asked.

Ashley felt her cheeks grow warm. "Just – just because," she mumbled.

She didn't want to tell her sister the truth – that today she was going to ask Taylor out on a date!

Ashley could imagine what Mary-Kate would say. "Are you nuts? Dad will never let you go out on a date! You're only eleven!"

Maybe he won't let me, Ashley thought. *But I'll*

cross that bridge when I come to it. If I come to it!

"There's only one little hole in the jersey," Mary-Kate argued. "In the sleeve. And anyway, I need to wear it. I have an important practice today – and this is my lucky jersey."

Lucky for you, maybe, Ashley thought. *But it's my tough luck if I have to wear it in front of Taylor!*

"I had this jersey on when I caught that fly ball at the Cubs game," Mary-Kate went on. "Remember?"

"I don't care if you were wearing it when you won the World Series!" Ashley wailed. "If I have to put it on when we change clothes, I'll die! Don't you get it?"

"No," Mary-Kate answered. "Not really."

Ashley's shoulders slumped. What good was it arguing with her sister? Mary-Kate just didn't understand how important it was to look great around boys.

She gave her sister one last desperate glance.

"Please? Just do it for me?" Ashley pleaded.

"Okay, okay," Mary-Kate gave in. "Tell you what. I'll lose the jersey – if you'll lose those pink tights. And that pink-striped knit dress."

"Deal," Ashley agreed. "I'll even do better than that. You can pick an outfit from my closet for me to wear to school. And I'll pick something from your closet for you. Then, when we change clothes, we'll both be happy!"

"Excellent!" Mary-Kate agreed with a smile.

Ashley hurried to Mary-Kate's closet and stared at the clothes hanging inside.

She bit her lip. This was going to be tough. Finding something pretty enough to impress Taylor – in this mess!

Finally she chose a purple T-shirt, a pair of stonewashed jeans, and purple socks to match.

"Here – wear this," Ashley told her sister.

Mary-Kate nodded, then handed Ashley a long, stretchy grey skirt and a teal sweater. "I guess I can live with these," Mary-Kate announced.

Great, Ashley thought. Now that she had the clothes part covered, she could concentrate on figuring out the next two steps.

First, how to ask Taylor for a date.

And second, how to handle it if he said no!

"Wow, Mary-Kate," Taylor said to Ashley that afternoon. "You're really flying through your maths homework. You didn't get a single problem wrong!"

Ashley played with her necklace – a purple string of beads. She had stuck it in her backpack and taken it to school to wear with the purple T-shirt outfit when she and Mary-Kate traded clothes.

"I owe it all, totally and completely, to you," she murmured, gazing into Taylor's eyes.

"I don't know." Taylor shook his head. "You even finished these problems about dividing fractions. But I didn't teach you that yet! Looks like you don't really need me."

"Oh, I definitely need you!" Ashley blurted out.

Taylor looked startled. He pushed his chair back from the table where they were working.

"What for?" he asked. "Decimals?"

"Not exactly," Ashley answered. Her heart began to beat faster.

"Well, what?" Taylor asked.

Okay, Ashley told herself. *This is it. This is my big chance to ask him for a date!*

She gave Taylor her sweetest smile and twirled her necklace again. She wished she didn't feel so breathless!

She drew in a deep, calming breath. "Well," she began. "You know that movie that just opened? *Headlong*? The one where the robot skyjacks the plane?"

"Yeah," Taylor said. "So what?"

"So I was wondering . . ."

Ashley felt her throat getting tight.

"Uh, I-I was wondering if you'd seen it yet," she finished, not quite coming to the point.

A smile spread across Taylor's face.

"Ohhhh," he said. "I get it – I know what you're asking."

"You do?" Ashley held her breath. Her heart pounded.

It was about to happen. He was going to say yes!

"Sure," Taylor answered. "You want to know if it's too violent for you, right? Or maybe you want me to tell your dad it's okay for you to see it. My mom is always doing that. She makes me go see movies first, so I can tell her if they're okay for my little sister."

No! Ashley thought. *What happened? That's not what I had in mind at all!*

Her mind whirled. What was she supposed to say now?

"Uh, you have a little sister?" she asked, scrambling to say something. Anything!

"Yeah – Mirabelle," Taylor answered. "Maybe you know her."

Ashley frowned. "I don't think so," she said. "What grade is she in?"

"Third," Taylor replied.

Oh, no! Ashley felt mortified. *I can't believe it.*

He's comparing me to a third grader!

"No, I'm positive I don't know her," Ashley insisted. "I mean, I'm much too busy with things like dates. With my busy social life, who has time to hang around with a bunch of little kids? You know?"

Taylor glanced at her sideways and shrugged. "Yeah, I guess," he said.

Good! Maybe he was finally getting the picture.

"So anyway, about the movie . . . " Ashley went on.

"You mean *Headlong?* Sorry. Haven't seen it," Taylor jumped in. "So I can't help you there."

"But that's just it!" Ashley said. "I haven't seen it either. So, uh, that makes two of us who haven't seen it."

"What's your point?" Taylor asked, wrinkling his forehead.

"M-my point?"

Ashley froze.

Just spit it out! she told herself. *Say it, before he decides you're a total idiot.*

But it wasn't that easy. Her mouth felt really dry all of a sudden. And her heart was pounding twice as hard.

This dating thing was rougher than it looked. Much, much rougher!

"Uh, my point is . . . I was wondering . . . I mean,

I-I was wondering if you were planning to go see it?" Ashley stammered.

"No way." Taylor shook his head. "It sounds really dumb. Don't you think?"

"Definitely," Ashley agreed, nodding her head quickly. "Exactly! That's what I was thinking, too. *Headlong* is way too dumb a movie for a date!"

"Date? Who said anything about a date?" Taylor asked, staring at her.

Ashley swallowed hard. "Uh, well, now that you mention it," she said, plunging ahead, "I was trying to come up with something fun to do. You know, on a date."

A broad smile spread across Taylor's face.

"Oh, I get it!" he said. "Why didn't you say so?"

Finally! Ashley thought. Her heart began to pound like a jackhammer again.

"You want me to help you come up with a date idea for you and a boy," Taylor guessed. "Is that it?"

No! No, no, no! Ashley could barely keep herself from banging her head on the table. Why, why was this going so wrong?

"Uh, not exactly," she managed. "Not a boy. A certain particular boy. A boy who's really good at maths. And who hangs around me after school . . . "

Hint, hint, Ashley thought. *Get it?*

59

Taylor's eyes opened wide.

"So that explains it!" he said with a laugh. "No wonder your maths homework was so good. You've got someone else tutoring you – cutting in on my time. How much is he getting paid?"

No! Ashley wanted to scream. *It's you! You're the one! You're the guy I want to go out with – more than anything in the world! Why aren't you getting it?*

But before she could think of anything else to say, Taylor started packing up his books.

"Listen, I've got to go. But here's what you do," he advised her. "Ask the guy to go rollerskating. That's always a good first date."

"So you like to skate?" Ashley asked quickly.

"Me?" Taylor said. "No way. I'm dangerous on any kind of wheels."

Then he headed towards the front door.

"Sorry for running out," he apologised. "I've got a Maths Team meeting. But you'll be fine on the make-up test – you're ready. So I'll see you tomorrow." He pulled the door open. "Oh, and Mary-Kate?" he added, flashing her a dazzling smile.

"Yes?" Ashley asked breathlessly.

"Do me a favour and don't tell your dad I cut out a few minutes early," Taylor said. "I really need to get paid for the full two hours."

And he pulled the door closed behind him.

Ashley sank back in her chair.

What a mess!

Her whole plan had totally fallen apart.

How did it happen? How could he miss all her signals? Ignore her hints?

There was only one explanation that made sense.

But it wasn't an explanation Ashley liked.

He's fifteen. I'm not even twelve yet. He would never even think of dating me, she realised. *To him, I'm just a little kid. Like his sister.*

She gazed down at the tabletop. For a moment she almost felt like crying.

I should give up on him, she told herself. *Just forget the whole thing and let Mary-Kate go back to being tutored.*

But then she shook her head.

"No," she said out loud. "It's too soon to give up. I just have to make him see how mature I am!"

Besides, as long as Taylor didn't realise she'd been chasing after him – and as long as he thought she was Mary-Kate and not Ashley – what did she have to lose?

CHAPTER
TEN

"Now remember, buddy," Eddie coached Kevin. "You're a good-looking guy with a great job and a terrific personality. Any girl would be lucky to have you! Now, which one is Stephanie?"

Kevin stepped away from the front door of the coffee bar. He lowered his voice so Stephanie wouldn't hear.

"Behind the counter," he said.

Eddie checked her out. So did Kevin, trying not to be too obvious about it.

Stephanie looked especially pretty today. She was wearing a tight blue ribbed sweater with skinny black stretch jeans. Her hair was loose around her shoulders, and she wore autumn-red lipstick.

"Whoa!" Eddie whistled under his breath. "Don't you think she's too pretty for you?"

Kevin gave Eddie a glare. "Why did I bring you?" he asked, exasperated.

"For support," Eddie said.

Kevin pointed to a table off to the side. "Support me from over there," he commanded.

Eddie made his way to the table. Kevin straightened his shirt and took a deep breath.

Well, here goes nothing, he thought.

But if it's nothing — why is my heart pounding as if I've just run the marathon?

Stephanie was just finishing serving a customer. *I'd better wait a minute more,* Kevin thought. *Who needs an audience? Just wait till the coast is clear — and then strike!*

He took another deep breath. Finally he walked up to the counter.

"Hi," he said, trying to sound normal and calm.

"Hey, Kevin," Stephanie answered cheerfully. "The usual?"

Kevin nodded. "And a regular drip," he added, remembering Eddie.

Stephanie started to get the coffees.

Okay, buddy, Kevin coached himself. *Just do it!*

He cleared his throat. "Listen, uh, Stephanie . . .

uh, you don't work nights, do you?" he asked.

Stephanie shook her head. "No, why?"

She handed him the two coffees and he gave her the money to pay for them.

"W-well," Kevin stammered, "I was thinking . . . we might have dinner sometime. You and I."

There. He said it. He asked her out!

So why is she just staring at me? Kevin wondered.

"You're asking me out?" Stephanie said flatly.

"Uh, yes." *What's wrong?* Kevin asked himself. He tried a smile. "I mean, there's a little place on the other side of campus. I've been wanting to try it, and— "

"I don't believe this!" Stephanie interrupted him. "You're the third guy to ask me out this morning!"

Is that good or bad? Kevin wondered. "Well, you do look very nice today," he began.

Stephanie shook her head. "You know, I thought you were different," she said. She sounded disappointed – and angry. "You always come in, get your coffee, never a problem. But I guess I was wrong."

Uh-oh, Kevin thought.

He glanced over his shoulder. A line was forming behind him. People wanted their coffee.

But they were also listening to what Stephanie

had to say – about him!

Kevin cleared his throat. "Uh – maybe I caught you at a bad time," he mumbled. "I'll just take my coffee and— "

"I mean, can't a single woman earn a living without being hit on?" Stephanie complained.

Kevin winced. Behind him he heard a woman say, "I know exactly how she feels!"

"Me, too," another woman agreed.

Kevin's face felt hot. He was so embarrassed! He had to say something to defend himself!

"But what about all those signals?" he blurted out, remembering what Carrie had said.

"Signals? What signals?" Stephanie demanded. She put her hands on her hips. Her eyes narrowed.

Kevin was starting to panic. *Why do I get the feeling that was exactly the wrong thing to say?* he asked himself.

"Well, I mean – you're always so nice to me. You even memorised my drink," he said feebly.

"You order the same thing every day!" Stephanie sputtered. "A monkey would know what you drink by now!"

Angrily, she whipped off her apron and balled it up. She tossed it on the counter. "That's it!" she announced. "I'm going on a break!"

And she stormed out the back door.

Kevin turned around and saw all the other customers glaring at him. They looked as if they wanted to choke him.

"Nice work, buddy," the man behind him snarled.

Kevin put a hand to his forehead. He felt about two inches tall.

No wonder I haven't asked anyone out since my wife died, he thought. *This whole dating thing is just too scary!*

Kevin grabbed his two coffees and hurried over to the table where Eddie was waiting.

"I saw the whole thing," Eddie said. "Ouch!"

"I don't suppose she's playing hard to get," Kevin said, looking hopefully at Eddie.

Eddie made a face. "If she is, she's pretty good at it!"

Kevin sat down and groaned.

This is all Carrie's fault, he thought. *If she hadn't put me up to this, I wouldn't be sitting here right now, feeling like a complete fool!*

He shook his head.

He didn't know how yet, but – someday, somehow, he was going to get back at her!

CHAPTER ELEVEN

"Taylor! You're just the man I'm looking for," Kevin Burke said as he walked in the front door.

He set his briefcase and the mail on a nearby table.

"Hey, Professor," Taylor called. "Mary-Kate's getting her books from her room. What's up?"

"I got a call from Mary-Kate's teacher today," Kevin announced. "She failed her make-up test."

Taylor looked totally shocked. "No way! She knows that material, Professor. Honestly!" he said.

Taylor strode over to the stairway and called up. "Hey, Mary-Kate, come on down here!"

Kevin and Taylor waited.

"Uh, I guess this would be a bad time to hit you up for a raise, huh, Professor?" Taylor mumbled.

"Very bad," Kevin agreed.

A moment later Ashley came bouncing down the stairs. Of course, she wasn't dressed like herself. She was wearing Mary-Kate's jeans and a basketball jersey – her usual outfit for her tutoring session with Taylor.

"Sorry for taking so long, Taylor," Ashley said, giving him a flirty smile. "I was trying something new with my hair." She twirled around so he could admire it.

As she spun, she noticed her dad standing across the room.

Whoops! She gulped.

Who knew Dad was home?

"Oh. Hi, Dad," Ashley mumbled. Was there any way she could fool him into thinking she was Mary-Kate?

"Hello, Ashley," Kevin replied. He folded his arms and stared at her. "Get dressed out of Mary-Kate's side of the closet today?"

Ashley giggled nervously. Uh-oh. Caught!

"Uh – Mary-Kate?" she called up the stairs. "I think you'd better come down here!"

From upstairs, Mary-Kate answered, "I thought I already was down there!"

"Well, you're not!" Ashley called sharply.

"But Dad is," she added.

Ashley checked out the look on her father's face – and swallowed hard. She knew that face. It meant big trouble.

But she was even more worried about the way Taylor was staring at her. As if . . . as if she were some sort of a jerk!

This is totally embarrassing, Ashley thought. *Now he's going to find out everything. How I've been chasing after him. How I was so desperate to be around him that I switched places with Mary-Kate.*

There was only one thing Ashley could do to save the situation.

Get out of there – fast!

"Well," she said, hurrying towards the front door, "Mary-Kate will be right down. See you later!"

She reached for the doorknob.

"Stick around, Ashley," Kevin said in his no-arguing voice. "This could be fun."

Fun? Ashley swallowed hard. Sure – about as much fun as sticking pins in your arm.

Actually – sticking pins in her arm might be a little more fun than what was about to happen!

She glanced up as Mary-Kate walked slowly down the stairs. Mary-Kate was wearing one of Ashley's outfits – a pair of blue stretch jeans with a blue and green top to match.

"Hi, Dad," Mary-Kate said. She went straight to the table. "Hey, Taylor. I can't wait to get started."

She's trying to bluff it out! Ashley realised. She held her breath. Could it possibly work?

"So where were we – chapter three?" Mary-Kate asked.

Chapter three? Ashley let out her breath with a whoosh. No. There was no way it could work!

"No, actually, we're on chapter seven," Taylor answered, giving Mary-Kate the same look he gave Ashley a moment ago.

"Seven?" Mary-Kate's eyes opened wide. "Boy, we're really flying!"

Kevin stepped forward. "Mary-Kate, the game is over," he declared. "Taylor, I'm afraid you've been tutoring the wrong student all week."

Ashley blushed and hung her head. Mary-Kate stared down at her feet.

"How could you two pull something like this?" Kevin demanded. "Especially you, Ashley."

Me? Why pick on me? Ashley wanted to say.

But she knew her dad was right. She had always realised, deep down, that switching places was wrong. That Mary-Kate needed to bring up her maths grades – and that she'd never do it without Taylor's help.

Still, she didn't want to admit the truth in front of Taylor! That would be too awful!

"Dad, could we talk about this in private?" Ashley asked, trying not to sound too desperate.

"No. I think Taylor deserves to hear why you've been wasting his time," Kevin said firmly.

Oh, boy, Ashley thought. *This is going to be mortifying!*

But there was no way around it. She had to tell the truth.

She turned so she didn't have to look at Taylor's face.

She took a deep breath. "Um, well, Dad, this is kind of embarrassing," she began. "You see, I kind of . . . well, I thought that if— "

"Dad," Mary-Kate interrupted, "this is all my fault."

Huh? Ashley shot a startled glance at her sister.

"Your fault?" Kevin asked.

"It was my idea," Mary-Kate announced. "I made Ashley do it so I could still make my basketball practices."

What's going on? Ashley wondered. *Why is Mary-Kate covering for me?*

Kevin didn't look convinced.

"And how did you do that?" he asked. "How did you make Ashley pull this switch?"

"I threatened to read her diary to everyone at school," Mary-Kate said.

"She doesn't keep a diary," Kevin stated.

"Oh, I would have written one for her," Mary-Kate shot back.

I don't believe this! Ashley thought. *Mary-Kate is the greatest sister! She totally saved me!*

Kevin still looked suspicious. But then he shook his head at both of them. "Okay. Ashley, I guess you can go upstairs. Mary-Kate, you start studying. We'll have a long talk about this later," he said.

He set his briefcase on the coffee table and began unloading papers from it.

"Professor? I'm still going to get paid for this week, right?" Taylor asked anxiously. "I mean, I was tutoring somebody."

Kevin sighed. "Relax, Taylor, you're getting paid," he answered.

Phew! Ashley thought. *At least Taylor isn't going to suffer because of what Mary-Kate and I did.*

Kevin glanced up and saw her still standing there. "Ashley, upstairs," he ordered.

Ashley started towards her room. But then she stopped. She needed an answer to something.

She pulled Mary-Kate aside.

"Why did you do that?" she whispered. "Why did you cover for me? You said if we got caught, I was on my own."

"I know." Mary-Kate shrugged. "But I just couldn't let you embarrass yourself in front of the man of your dreams."

Ashley gave her sister a quick hug. "Thanks! I owe you big-time."

"Oh, you have no idea!" Mary-Kate replied. "Big-time doesn't even begin to describe it." She grinned.

"Ashley, you're my slave for life!"

CHAPTER TWELVE

Carrie pushed open the kitchen door – and spotted Kevin Burke standing at the counter, sorting through the day's mail. His back was turned to her.

"Junk . . . junk . . . junk . . ." he muttered. Then he stopped and held up a fistful of catalogues. "I don't believe this!" he complained. "They sent me two of these. Two exactly alike!"

Carrie grinned. "They must know you have twins," she joked.

Kevin jumped and spun around. When he noticed Carrie, his already-sour expression got even sourer.

He looks as if he just bit into a very large lemon, Carrie thought.

"Where have you been?" Kevin asked.

"Oh, I thought the girls would be okay on their own," Carrie answered. "So I went to shoot some pool and have a few drinks."

Kevin just stared at her.

Uh-oh, Carrie thought. *It must be a really bad day.* "I took the trash out," she explained with a sigh.

"Thank you," Kevin said in an icy voice. He turned back to sorting the mail.

Carrie studied him as she put a new plastic bag in the garbage can. There was something she wanted to bring up. But she didn't know quite how to do it. Especially when he seemed to be in such a rotten mood already!

Oh, well. Plunge right in! Carrie thought. That's what she usually did anyway.

"Listen," she said, softening her voice. "I, uh, heard about what happened at the coffee bar. With Stephanie."

"Oh, thank you for that, too," Kevin snapped. "I suppose Eddie told you?"

"Well, actually, a couple of guys from my English Lit class were there," Carrie admitted.

"Oh, terrific! Did they hear what happened? Or did they just – how did you put it – 'read the signals'?" he asked grumpily.

75

"All right. I get the point," Carrie said. She tilted her head to one side. "I might have made a mistake."

Kevin's eyes popped open wide. "Might have? I've got twenty coffee-drinking witnesses who saw me crash and burn!" he complained.

"Okay, okay, I blew it and I'm sorry," Carrie apologised. She really was sorry, too. "I was just trying to help."

And then Kevin did something that really surprised her. He nodded.

"I know," he said. "And you know what? In your own bizarre way, you did help."

"Really?" Carrie held her breath. What exactly did he mean? Was he setting her up for another nasty crack – or was he being sincere?

"Yeah. Because of you, I asked a woman out and she turned me down," Kevin said. "At first I was mortified – and mad at you, too. I was trying to think of some way to get back at you." He shrugged. "But then, as I was standing here, I realised – hey, this could be a good thing."

"You're one of those guys who always thinks the glass is half-full, not half-empty, aren't you?" Carrie guessed.

Kevin shrugged again. "Maybe so. See, it's been a long time," he explained. "So I was nervous about asking someone out. And afraid of being rejected. Thanks to you, I got both those things out of the way at once. And I didn't even have to buy her dinner!"

"Well . . . " Carrie watched his face closely. Hmmm. He really didn't look too upset! "I'm glad I could help."

"Of course, there is a down side," Kevin went on.

"What?" Carrie asked, instantly suspicious.

"Now I have to find a new coffee place," Kevin announced. He flashed her a slight smile. Picking up his mail, he walked out of the room.

Carrie watched him leave. She noticed that his hair was messed up at the back. In sort of a cute way.

He's definitely date material, she thought. Even if Stephanie didn't want to go out with him – he should try again with someone else.

I know he doesn't want me butting in – but he needs me. I'm going to find the right woman for him, Carrie vowed to herself. *Even if it takes a long time.*

And even if he kills me in the process!

CHAPTER THIRTEEN

"Don't you see, Mary-Kate? You can't add decimals and fractions together. There's no way," Taylor explained. "So you have to change the fraction to a decimal – and then add them together."

The two of them sat in a corner of the living room, working hard.

"I like fractions better," Mary-Kate moaned. "Can't I do it the other way?"

"You mean change the decimal to a fraction?" Taylor asked.

Mary-Kate nodded.

Taylor sighed. "Well, you could," he agreed. "But just what fraction would you make out of 4.835712?"

"Uh, maybe . . . "

Mary-Kate stared at the page. Her eyes felt really blurry. In fact, her whole head felt blurry!

"How about if we just use a calculator and forget the whole thing?" she suggested.

"We are using calculators," Taylor reminded her.

"Oh, yeah," Mary-Kate sighed. "Well, they aren't making this any easier!"

"Tell you what," Taylor said. "I think we need a break. Or a snack – or something. You've been concentrating too long. Got any microwave popcorn?"

"Yes!" Mary-Kate agreed, jumping up from the table and giving him a high five.

Mary-Kate got out a bag of popcorn and stuck it in the microwave. As it was popping, she poured glasses of soda for Taylor and herself. Then she carried the goodies to the table.

If Dad sees us snacking this close to dinner, he'll have a fit, she thought.

But she didn't care. She had to do something to clear her head! Otherwise, she'd never catch on to those maths problems.

Please, just let me learn fractions and decimals by tomorrow, Mary-Kate prayed. Tomorrow was the last day of practice before the big game. She had to show up for that if she wanted to be on the starting team.

If I get all of these problems right, maybe Dad will let me quit being tutored! Mary-Kate thought.

But what were the chances?

Mary-Kate munched the popcorn and took a sip of soda. "Okay, show me again," she said, sitting back down at the table.

"I've got a better idea," Taylor said. "I'm going to draw you a picture."

He took out a blank sheet of paper and drew a basketball court. Then he drew five stick figures on the court.

"Those are the players," Taylor explained. "Now pretend two of them are hurt. They can't play. That's two out of five – or two-fifths. Right?"

Mary-Kate beamed. Taylor really was a good tutor. He had a million different ways to explain things. If she didn't understand it one way, he came up with another.

Taylor kept drawing basketball players. Mary-Kate nodded and worked on her problems. After ten more minutes it began to sink in.

She was getting it!

"Way to go!" Taylor said, after he checked her work. "You got the first four problems right! Keep going."

Mary-Kate looked ahead in the book.

"Only twenty-six more problems to do," Taylor said encouragingly.

Mary-Kate groaned. Suddenly she didn't feel so hopeful. "Twenty-six? Ugh! I'll never make it."

She copied another problem on to her scratch paper. But before she could start on it, the phone rang.

Mary-Kate jumped up to answer it. "Hello?" she said into the phone.

Max's voice came over the line. "Mary-Kate, where were you today? You missed basketball practice."

"Don't rub it in," Mary-Kate grumbled. "My dad came home early and caught on to our switching-places trick. So I had to stay home for tutoring."

"Well, you'd better show up tomorrow," Max warned. "We need you. And Coach Martin put Tanya Morris in your spot today."

"He replaced me already?" Mary-Kate gasped. "You've got to be kidding!"

"Just for today's practice," Max said. "But he might make it permanent."

Mary-Kate gripped the phone tighter.

"What did he say?" she asked. "I mean, did he say I was definitely off the team?"

"No," Max answered. "But Tanya told him you were giving up basketball to devote your life to maths."

"Give me a break!" Mary-Kate cried. "She's just

jealous because I've got a decent jump shot and she doesn't. She's trying to get me kicked off the team!"

"Well, it's working!" Max informed her.

Biting her lip, Mary-Kate glanced at Taylor. He was drumming his fingers on the table and checking his watch.

"I've got to go, Max," Mary-Kate said. "But don't worry. I'll be at practice tomorrow – somehow!"

She hung up and hurried back to her schoolbooks.

But Taylor pushed away from the table and stood up.

"That's my two hours," he said. He started packing up his things. "Do you think you can handle the rest of the homework problems by yourself?"

By myself? Mary-Kate thought. *No way!* "Can't you just stay another twenty minutes?" she pleaded. "I'll pay you myself – somehow. Do you take coupons?"

Taylor laughed. "Sorry," he said. "I've got another tutoring appointment with another, uh, tutee – or whatever you call yourself. So I'll see you tomorrow. Good luck!"

He hurried out the door.

"Tutee? Uh-uh," Mary-Kate moaned when he was gone. "I call myself dead meat!"

For a minute, she just stared at the twenty-six remaining maths problems. Why did Miss Tandy have to give so much homework every night?

Ashley's voice came from behind her. "Mary-Kate?"

"What?" Mary-Kate snapped, turning around.

"Don't bite my head off!" Ashley said, holding up her hands. "I just came down to help."

"You? Help?" Mary-Kate asked. She wrinkled her nose. She wasn't exactly in the mood to spend time with Ashley.

I never should have listened to her in the first place, Mary-Kate thought. *If I hadn't switched places with her, I would have learned fractions and decimals by now! Taylor's tutoring would have paid off. My maths grade would have improved – and I would be able to go back to basketball practise tomorrow.*

But in her heart Mary-Kate knew she wasn't being fair. It wasn't Ashley's fault. Mary-Kate had wanted to switch places just as much as Ashley did. She'd been thrilled to get out of the tutoring.

She unwrinkled her nose. "Help me how?" she asked.

"With your maths homework – duh!" Ashley answered. "I mean, you aren't sitting there wishing someone would give you a manicure, are you?"

Mary-Kate laughed. "Will you really help me?"

"Sure," Ashley said. "Come on upstairs and I'll teach you my secret about thirds."

"Thanks!" Mary-Kate cried.

Maybe, just maybe, if she got all of her homework right, her dad would let her play basketball tomorrow. She crossed her fingers – on both hands – for good luck.

Both hands. That should be twice as much good luck, Mary-Kate thought.

But would it be enough?

CHAPTER FOURTEEN

"This is great, Mary-Kate!" Kevin said. He sat on the end of her bed, looking at her maths homework. "I'm proud of you. See? All you have to do is apply yourself."

Mary-Kate pulled her knees up to her chest and smiled. She was wearing her favourite pyjama outfit – grey knit shorts and a maroon basketball jersey. Ashley sat on her own bed, wearing silky pink pyjamas.

"I guess Taylor's a pretty good tutor," Mary-Kate commented. "He sure taught me a lot."

She gave Ashley a sly look. "And he's cute, too. Don't you agree, Ashley?"

Ashley felt her cheeks growing warm. She shot

Mary-Kate a warning glance. "I hadn't noticed," she mumbled.

"So anyway, Dad," Mary-Kate went on, "since I got all of my homework right, can we make a deal?"

"What kind of a deal?" Kevin asked. He sounded reluctant.

"A deal about maths and basketball," Mary-Kate said. "Because I'm one-fifth of the team, remember?"

Ashley rolled her eyes. Mary-Kate was really laying on the maths-talk thick!

"But if I don't show up for practice tomorrow," Mary-Kate went on, "I'm going to be one-fifth of nothing!"

Kevin laughed. "That's not true, Mary-Kate. You'll still be on the team."

"No, I won't, Dad," Mary-Kate declared. "At least, I won't be on the starting team – not if I miss tomorrow's practice. And I won't get to play in the big game on Saturday, either."

Kevin looked thoughtful. "I see your point. So what do you have in mind?"

"I was thinking of a sixty-forty split," Mary-Kate suggested. "I go to basketball every Monday, Wednesday, and Friday, and get tutored every Tuesday and Thursday. What do you say?"

Hmmm, Ashley thought. That way, Taylor would

come over less than half as often as before. That was bad.

But, on the other hand, Mary-Kate wouldn't improve on her maths as quickly if she didn't have a tutoring session every day.

So Taylor would have to stick around for weeks and weeks!

That was good. Very good!

Ashley felt a broad smile stretching across her face. *That will give me another chance to win him over*, she realised. *As myself!*

Kevin thought about it for a minute.

"All right," he finally said. "It's a deal. But I'm still not happy about you two switching places. And that was your idea, right, Mary-Kate?"

Ashley held her breath. But Mary-Kate didn't even hesitate. "Yes," she said firmly. "Sorry," she added.

"Sorry's not enough," Kevin said. "When you get home from basketball tomorrow, you'll have to clean the attic and sweep out the basement. And after that you'll be cooking dinner."

Mary-Kate hung her head. "Okay," she said softly.

Wow, Ashley thought. *That's a lot of work!*

"Dad, don't you think you're being a little hard

on Mary-Kate?" she asked.

"After what she pulled? No, Ashley, I don't. Good night, girls," Kevin said, and left the room.

When he was gone, Mary-Kate glanced at Ashley. "Cleaning the attic," she moaned dramatically. "Sweeping the basement. Cooking dinner!"

Then she flashed Ashley a huge grin. "Looks like you've got a busy day tomorrow, Cinderella!"

Ashley let out a sigh. *I guess I saw that coming,* she thought.

And to tell the truth, she had to admit it was fair.

After all, Mary-Kate did take all the blame for Ashley's idea.

Ashley let her head sink into her pillow.

Oh, well. Doing all those chores was a small price to pay for having such a great sister. A sister who would take the heat for you when things got rough.

And besides, Ashley thought with a smile, *there is one good thing about this arrangement.*

If I'm Cinderella, then I'll wind up with the prince in the end!

Mary-Kate & Ashley's Scrapbook

We were playing
house hockey in
the living room . . .

. . . when Dad walked in and announced
that he'd got Mary-Kate a maths tutor.
That's where the trouble started.

When the tutor walked through the door, Ashley couldn't believe her eyes. His name was Taylor...

... and that night Ashley decided he was the
cutest boy she'd ever seen!

But how could we get
him to notice Ashley?

We did a switcheroo on him!

Did it work?

Well, not
exactly . . .

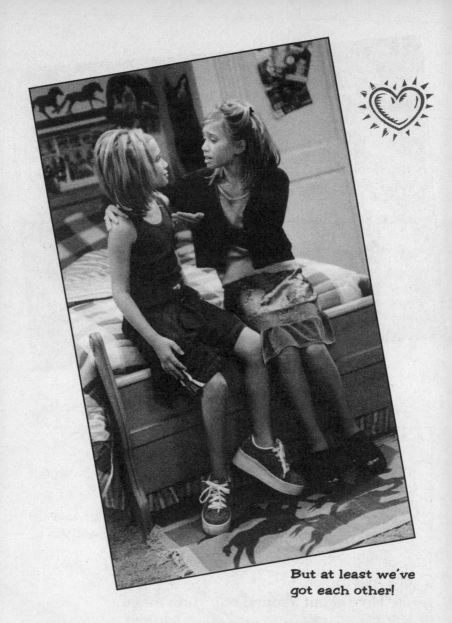

But at least we've
got each other!

The Sleepover Secret

"So what do you want to play now, Jennifer?"
Mary-Kate asked.

She straightened her Chicago Cubs sleepshirt and
looked around the attic. She and Ashley used it as
their private hangout. The floor was covered with
sleeping bags, bowls of snacks, and piles of clothes.

So far, Ashley's sleepover is going great, Mary-Kate
thought. *Even though Jennifer Dilber is here.* Jennifer
was the most popular girl in Mary-Kate and
Ashley's class. Ashley thought she was cool. Mary-
Kate thought she was a real pain.

Jennifer tilted her head as she looked at each girl
one by one.

"How about a round of… truth or dare?"

"Truth or dare?" Ashley repeated.

"Oh, great," Mary-Kate grumbled. She hated

truth or dare!

Jennifer smiled. "Is everyone in?"

Mary-Kate watched as Ashley's friends nodded.

"Sure, Jennifer," Ashley said cheerfully. "Let the game begin."

"Cool," Jennifer said. "You go first."

"Why me?" Ashley gulped.

"Alphabetical order," Jennifer explained. "Okay, Ashley. Truth or dare?"

Mary-Kate glanced at her sister. What would it be?

"Truth!" Ashley said with a smile.

Jennifer gave it a thought. Then she grinned.

"Okay, Ashley," she said. "If you had to spend the rest of your life on a deserted island with only one boy, who would it be?"

"Oh, that's easy," Ashley said. She gave Mary-Kate a little wink. "The answer is . . . Taylor Donovan."

"Who's Taylor Donovan?" Jennifer asked. She looked excited.

"My maths tutor," Mary-Kate offered.

"He's fifteen," Ashley added. "He has his own band, and his cousin was on *Jeopardy*!"

"Fifteen?" Amanda squealed.

"An older guy!" Darcy gasped.

Mary-Kate looked around the attic. The girls seemed interested – except Jennifer. She just looked bored.

"A maths tutor, huh? Okay, okay." Jennifer sighed.

She pointed to Mary-Kate. "You're next, Mary-Kate."

"But my name begins with M!" Mary-Kate protested. "You go before I do!"

Ashley nudged her sister. "Just do it."

"No," Mary-Kate said. "I'm not playing."

"What's the matter?" Jennifer snickered. "Are you chicken? Cluck! Cluck! Cluck!"

Mary-Kate glared at Jennifer. No way would she let Miss High-and-Mighty make her look like a wimp!

"Fine!" Mary-Kate snapped. "Truth."

"This is going to be good," Jennifer said. She rubbed her hands together.

"Okay, Mary-Kate. What's the most you ever did with a boy?" she asked.

The sound of ooohs and woos filled the attic.

So she wants the truth, huh? Mary-Kate thought.
Okay – I'll give her the truth.
Let's see if she can handle it!

to be continued...

mary-kateandashley

TWO of a kind ™

Coming soon – can you collect them all?

HarperCollins*Entertainment*

PARACHUTE PRESS

DUALSTAR PUBLICATIONS

mary-kateandashley.com
AOL Keyword: mary-kateandashley

TM & © 2002 Dualstar Entertainment Group, Inc.

mary-kateandashley

Meet Chloe and Riley Carlson.

So much to do...

so little time

(1)	How to Train a Boy	(0 00 714458 X)
(2)	Instant Boyfriend	(0 00 714448 2)
(3)	Too Good to be True	(0 00 714449 0)
(4)	Just Between Us	(0 00 714450 4)
(5)	Tell Me About It	(0 00 714451 2)
(6)	Secret Crush	(0 00 714452 0)

... and more to come!

HarperCollins*Entertainment*

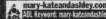

Order Form

To order direct from the publishers, just make a list of the titles you want and fill in the form below:

Name ....

Address ....

....

....

Send to: Dept 6, HarperCollins Publishers Ltd, Westerhill Road, Bishopbriggs, Glasgow G64 2QT.

Please enclose a cheque or postal order to the value of the cover price, plus:

UK & BFPO: Add £1.00 for the first book, and 25p per copy for each additional book ordered.

Overseas and Eire: Add £2.95 service charge. Books will be sent by surface mail but quotes for airmail despatch will be given on request.

A 24-hour telephone ordering service is available to holders of Visa, MasterCard, Amex or Switch cards on 0141- 772 2281.

Collins
An *Imprint* of HarperCollins*Publishers*